Deborah Niland

When I Was a Baby

Puffin Baby

and crawled everywhere.

I had two teeth.

I ate mushy stuff.

I snuggled in my blanket,

and I loved cuddles.

Now
I am a
big boy.

I can run and jump.

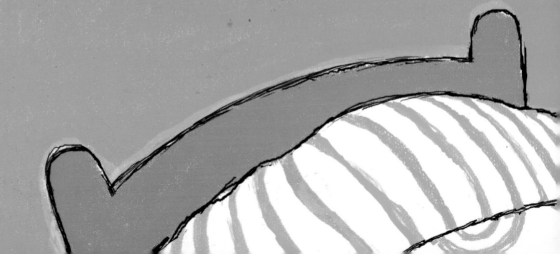

I have lots of teeth.

I have a new baby sister.

I gave her my blanket.

I still love cuddles.